John Burningham

ALDO

Crown Publishers, Inc.
New York

Other books by John Burningham

Granpa
Where's Julius?
John Patrick Norman McHennessy
   — the boy who was always late
Humbert, Mister Firkin and
   the Lord Mayor of London
Hey! Get Off Our Train

Library of Congress Cataloging-in-Publication Data
Burningham, John. Aldo / John Burningham.   p.   cm. Summary: A small girl reflects on the comfort she
gets from her imaginary friend Aldo.
[1. Imaginary playmates—Fiction.]   I. Title.
PZ7.B936A1 1992   [E]—dc20   91-19589
ISBN 0-517-58701-7 (trade).
    0-517-58699-1 (lib. bdg.)

10 9 8 7 6 5 4 3 2 1

First American Edition

I spend a lot of time on my own.

Of course I watch television,

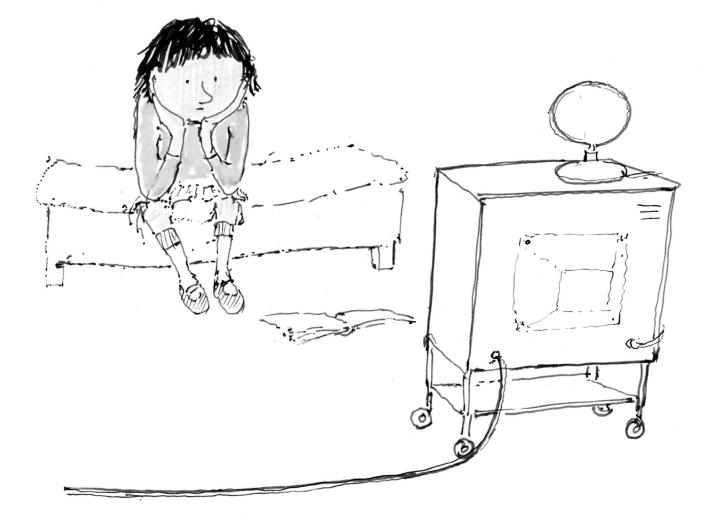

and I have lots of toys and books
and things.

Sometimes we go to the park,

and occasionally we go out to eat,

which is nice.

But then I'm on my own again.

I'm lucky, though. I'm really very, very lucky, because I have a special friend.

His name is Aldo.

Aldo is only friends with me, and he's a secret.
I know he will always come to me
when things get really bad.

Like when they were horrible to me
the other day.

I'm sure they went away
because Aldo came.

Aldo takes me to wonderful places.
I'm not scared of anything
when I'm with Aldo.

I couldn't ever tell anybody about Aldo.
They would never believe me,
and they would just laugh.

Sometimes I wish he could help,
but he's only my special friend.

Once I woke up in the night after
a bad dream and Aldo was not there,
and I thought he would never
come to see me ever again.

But Aldo had only gone to get a story,
which he read to me until I went to sleep.

I wish Aldo could be with me all the time.

Of course, there are some days
when I forget all about him,
but I know that if things get really bad...

Aldo will always be there.